# SEVEN SIMEONS

# SEVEN SIMEONS

## A RUSSIAN TALE

### RETOLD AND ILLUSTRATED

### BY BORIS ARTZYBASHEFF

NEW YORK · THE VIKING PRESS · MCMXXXVII

FIRST PUBLISHED APRIL 1937


COPYRIGHT 1937 BY BORIS ARTZYBASHEFF

PUBLISHED BY THE VIKING PRESS, INC.

PRINTED IN THE UNITED STATES OF AMERICA

BY QUINN & BODEN COMPANY, INC., RAHWAY, N. J.

DISTRIBUTED IN CANADA BY THE MACMILLAN

COMPANY OF CANADA, LTD.

# SEVEN SIMEONS

Beyond the high mountains and the dark forests, beyond the great rivers and the blue seas, in a certain kingdom upon a certain flat place, stood a city. In this city lived a king and the king's name was Douda.

King Douda was wise, King Douda was rich, and he was strong, for he had a strong army; so strong it was that nobody knew just how strong, not even his own generals.

Of big cities he had forty times forty, with ten palaces in each, each with a silver door, crystal windows, and a roof of gold, and of the best gold, too!

To advise him in matters of state he had nine old men, all with long white beards and large wise heads, all with more brains than enough; they always told him the truth!

Would you not think that a king like Douda should have been happy? Not at all! There he was: rich, wise, powerful, and, moreover, he was very good-looking! So good-looking was King Douda that his beauty could not be imagined, nor described with a pen, nor told about in a tale. Yet he was very unhappy. He was sad because he could not find a worthy maiden for a bride, a princess who would be as good-looking as himself.

Once as he sat on a golden chair in his garden upon the shores of the sea, thinking about his misfortune, he saw a ship sail up to the dock before his palace. The sailors dropped anchor, furled their sails, and then laid a plank to come ashore.

King Douda thought to himself: "The sailors sail upon many seas and see marvels quite unknown. I shall ask them if in their travels they have not heard of some princess who is as good-looking as myself."

The sailors were brought to the King and they bowed before him in the best manner. A cup of wine was served to them; when they had drunk the wine and wiped their beards, King Douda said to them:

"It is well known that you sail upon the seas and see many marvels.

Now tell us in all truth and honesty, isn't there some king or mighty prince who has a daughter as good-looking as myself? For King Douda to be a worthy bride, for this great kingdom to be a worthy queen?"

The sailors thought and then thought some more; then the eldest one said, "Aye, I have heard that far beyond the distant sea, upon an island, there is a mighty kingdom. And the king has a daughter, Princess Helena, who is as good-looking as yourself. But this fair maiden is not a bride for you!"

Here the King became angry. "How dare you speak so to me, King Douda? Where is this island, what is the name of it, and who knows the way there?"

"It is called Boozan Island, and it is not near," replied the mariner. "Ten years of travel by the watery way, and the way to it we do not know. But even should we know it, judge for yourself. Ten years sailing there, ten years sailing back, adds twenty. By that time the fair lady will age, and girlish beauty is not like the taxpayer's duty: it's here today but gone tomorrow."

King Douda became pensive. "Well," he said, "it's to my sorrow. But as a reward for you, sailors, I give you a grant. You may take your ship to any part of my kingdom and pay neither tax nor duty!"

The sailors bowed low and departed, but the King sat there on his golden chair, in the garden upon the shores of the sea, thinking. And his thoughts were like entangled black threads. He could never find the end to them.

Douda was sad, but then he thought, "If I go hunting and have some fun, I may lose my sorrow in the fields; in the dark forest I might drop it. Then by tomorrow I might think how I could marry this beautiful princess."

The King's huntsmen blew their horns loud, the King's horsemen came galloping out, and King Douda rode forth to hunt, to forget his sorrow and to have some fun.

They were riding over the plains and through the dark forests, up the hills, and down the valleys looking for white geese and swans, for black bears and red foxes, when suddenly they came upon a beautiful field of wheat, shining like gold in the sun. When his hunting party had galloped through the field, King Douda reined in his horse and looked back in admiration.

"That is very fine wheat," he said. "One can see that the man who tilled this soil must be a good worker. Should all the fields throughout my kingdom be plowed and seeded like this one, there would be so much bread that my people could never eat it up, even in a lifetime!"

And King Douda ordered that the man who plowed the field should

be found. The King's horsemen galloped off to do as they were told and shortly came upon seven youths sitting under a tree. Goodly lads they were, dressed in white linen shirts, themselves very handsome and so much alike that you could not tell them apart. They sat in the shade eating their dinner, a loaf of rye bread and plenty of good, clear, spring water.

"Hey, whose field is this here, with the golden wheat shining in the sun?"

"Ours!" said the seven in one voice. "By us plowed and by us seeded."

"And who may you fellows be, and whose people?"

"We are subjects of our good King Douda. To each other we are brothers; by name we are called Simeon."

The King's horsemen rode back and took the seven brothers with them, so that the King could see them for himself. The King liked the brothers and spoke to them very kindly, asking them who they were, and why and how.

"We are simple folk," said the first Simeon, "and your peasants, Douda. To each other we are brothers by the same father of the same mother, and the name we answer to is Simeon. Our old father taught us to pray to God; to serve our King faithfully; to pay our taxes regularly; and to till the soil without surcease. 'If you, my sons, aren't lazy,' he said, 'if you plow the soil in the proper way and seed it in the right season, it will reward you. It will give bread for you to eat and, when the time comes and you are old and tired, it will make a soft place for your rest.' Our father also told us to learn different trades. 'A craft,' said father, 'is not a heavy burden, but it is good to know one against a rainy day. The best aid is some useful trade,' he said."

King Douda was pleased with their simple speech.

"Good fellows!" he said. "Very good fellows! And what may be the trades you have learned from your father?"

Answered the first Simeon,

"Mine is a simple one. If I should be given the right tools and plenty of bricks, I can build a tower higher than the clouds, almost to the very sky."

"Good!" said the King. "Let's hear from the others."

Answered the second Simeon,

"My skill isn't much. Should my brother build this tower, I could climb to the top of it and from there I could see all the kingdoms of the world. I could tell what's going on in every one of them."

"This is very good," said the King. "And the next?"

Answered the third Simeon,

"My trade is an easy one. When you, Douda, need ships for your

royal navy they are built by real masters, men of great learning and experience. But should you order me, I shall take an axe and go to it: slap, dash, a tap and a clout, and your ship is turned out! But then, my ship would be a crude, home-made thing. While the real ship takes a year to sail, mine is back in an hour; while the real ship takes ten years to sail, mine is there in a week. Such an artless, crude thing this ship would be."

"Very nice," said the King. "And what about you?"

Answered the fourth Simeon,

"My trade is easy! Should my brother build this ship, I could sail it to the ends of the earth. And if some enemy starts after it or a great storm breaks out over the sea, I shall make the ship go down, I shall hide it deep down below, in the watery depths. But when the danger is over I can bring it up again upon the blue waters of the sea."

"Not bad," said the King. "However, I have heard of it being done in our Navy, the first part of it at any rate. Next!"

Answered the fifth Simeon,

"My trade is that of a simple blacksmith. If you should give me a scrap of iron, I can fashion a gun for you. This gun will shoot by itself and never miss."

"Splendid!" said the King. "But, please, go on."

Answered the sixth Simeon,

"Of my skill I am ashamed to tell. If my brother shoots anything I can always recover it. Be it in the sky or in the forest, be it in the deep sea or behind a cloud, I shall go down, I shall climb up and always bring back what the gun shoots."

"Dear me! This is the best of all," said King Douda, because he was very much pleased with the Simeons' modesty. "Our thanks to you all for your good, simple words. It is true, what your father has told you, 'A craft is not a heavy burden, but it is good to know one against a rainy day.' Come with me to my City. I wish to see for myself what you can do."

The seven Simeons bowed low before Douda, and said in one voice, "You are our high and mighty Douda and if such be your pleasure we are your humble servants."

But the King remembered the seventh brother. "And you, Simeon, what is the trade you have learned from your father?"

Answered the seventh Simeon,

"I have learned nothing from him! Not that I haven't tried, but it flew into one ear and out of the other. I do have some skill in one thing, but I would rather not mention it."

"Speak!" exclaimed King Douda. "What is this secret thing?"

"No, Douda! First I must have your promise, your royal pledge

that after I've told you, you will forgive me and let me keep my head in the same place it is now."

"Be it so!" said the King. "I give you my royal word."

The seventh Simeon looked around, stepped from foot to foot, coughed, and then spoke,

"My talent, King Douda, should remain hidden, because instead of its being rewarded, men's heads are chopped off for such ability. My skill is this: there isn't a treasure, be it concealed, locked up or buried, be it behind a door, a lock, or a bar, that I cannot have, should I take a fancy to it."

"What's that?" exclaimed King Douda. "I will not put up with it, it's too grave a matter!"

The King was very displeased and angry. "No, there is no excuse for a thief, no mercy for such a vicious villain. I shall have you put to death; I shall lock you up in the darkest dungeon and keep you there behind iron bars till you forget this skill!"

"But, King Douda, you have heard the old saying, 'He who is not caught, is not a thief.' If I had my fancy I could have even your kingdom's treasury. With all its gold I could have a palace built as good as your own! But such is my simplicity, that my only guilt is that I am telling you the truth."

"This is a most provoking situation," the King said. "I have given you my royal pledge, but to let you go free is to ask for trouble. You must be, for safety, locked up. Hey, jailors, take this man, clamp irons upon him and toss him into the darkest dungeon. From this day forward he is not to see the light of day, nor the bright sun nor the silver moon.

"As for you other Simeons, you are in my favor. Come with me and do what you were taught by your father, so that I can see it for myself."

The six Simeons went to the King's City as they were told, but the seventh was locked in a dark, damp place.

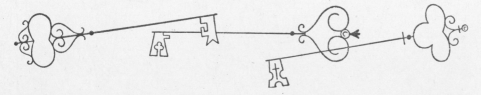

When they came to the city, the first Simeon was promptly given plenty of bricks and the proper tools to set to work. The tower grew up so fast and so high that the King, as he was looking at it, had to hold his crown with one hand and shade his eyes with the other. It almost reached to the sun.

The second Simeon, when the tower was ready, climbed to the top

of it. He looked East, North, West and South, and he listened. Then he came down and told what was going on in the world, which king was fighting a war, which king was planning a war, and which one had had enough and was suing for peace. Then, besides, he told of such secret things that the King smiled and his Court laughed themselves blue in the face.

The third Simeon lost no time. He rolled up his sleeves, took an axe and went to work. Slap, dash, a tap and a clout, and the ship was turned out! When King Douda rode to the shore to see it, the ship's flags waved, silken sails were blown full by the wind, and the brass cannons fired the salute. But what was best, the ship had silver strings for its rigging and the sailors played good music on it. The fourth Simeon sailed the ship upon the blue waters. When it was out in the open sea, he took it by its carved prow and made it go down like a stone! It seemed as if there never had been a ship upon the water, but an hour later he brought it up again, and a nice big fish, besides, for the King's supper.

While King Douda was amusing himself with the ship, the fifth Simeon had his smithy ready, the iron hot, and before long he had fashioned the gun, the gun which shoots by itself and never misses!

There was an eagle flying high in the sky. It flew up to the sun and was looking at it. The King spoke to the fifth brother,

"See," he said, "if you can shoot that foolish bird. It flies, looking at the sun, as if there were nothing better to do!"

The fifth Simeon only smiled. He loaded his gun with a silver bullet, aimed—bang! And the eagle came tumbling down head first and legs last. But before it fell to the ground the sixth Simeon caught it on a silver platter and brought it to the King.

"I like that!" said the King. "That was very well done and we are much pleased with you and your brothers. We shall reward you. To show our appreciation you may go to the royal kitchen to rest and have a good dinner."

The six Simeons bowed low and went to the kitchen as they were told. But just as they began to eat their soup, the King's jester came rushing in waving his cap with little bells on it.

"Here, here, you blockheads!" the Jester cried. "You country bumpkins! A fine time you pick out to eat your dinner. Come, King Douda is asking for you!"

The brothers ran to the King's chambers. What great disaster could have happened? They saw standing by the door all the King's men, his Sergeants, Lieutenants, Major-Generals, Senators, and the Best People. The King himself sat on his golden chair looking pensive.

"Listen," he said to the Simeons, "I am very pleased with you, my

good fellows. But my Generals and my Senators had a thought. If you, second Simeon, can see the world from the top of your tower, you must go up and look. For I am told that somewhere beyond the Great Sea is an island. On this island is a king and the king has a daughter. I am told that this princess is as good-looking as myself."

The second Simeon ran to the tower without delay. From the tower he looked this way and that way, then came down and reported.

"King Douda, your command I have carried out. I looked beyond the Great Sea and I saw Boozan Island. From what I see the king there is very proud and unfriendly. He sits in his palace and talks like this: 'I have a daughter, beautiful Helena, and nowhere in the world is there a king or a prince worthy of her hand. Should one come here to woo her, I would declare war on him! I would chop off his head and burn his kingdom to ashes!' "

"But how big is his army?" asked Douda. "And how far is his kingdom from my kingdom?"

"To make a rough guess, to sail there would take ten years less two days, but should a storm break out it might take a bit longer. I did see the king's army, too. It was training in the field, but there were not many: a hundred thousand lancers, a hundred thousand gunners, and of his horsemen about the same number. The king also has another army in reserve. It never goes any place but is fed and groomed for some emergency."

King Douda thought very long, then exclaimed,

"I do want to marry beautiful Helena!" After he had exclaimed this the Generals and Senators kept silent and only tried to hide behind each other's backs.

"If I may speak, Sir," said the third Simeon, and he coughed a little. "I would say, Sir, but I am only a simple man and have no education, I would say, that although my ship is a crude, home-made thing, it could bring the Princess. While the real ship takes a year to sail, mine is back in an hour; while the real ship takes ten years to sail, mine would be there in a week."

"Now we are getting somewhere!" said Douda. "Hey, my brave Generals and wise Senators, think quickly! Should I, your King Douda, win beautiful Helena by war or shall we first try diplomacy? I now give you my promise that he who brings her to me shall be in my favor. He shall be made the Lord High Keeper of the Kingdom's Treasury and can help himself to it!"

All were silent as before, and there was a shuffling of feet as the Generals and Senators tried to hide behind each other's backs. King Douda frowned and was about to speak an angry word to them when, as if someone had asked for it, the King's Jester jumped forward. The

Jester shook his cap with the little golden bells on it and exclaimed,

"Here, here, you wise men! Your heads are big, your beards are long but all your brains aren't worth a song. Have you, King Douda, forgotten the old saying, that sometimes even the prickly thorn, for an ass might serve as corn? The seventh Simeon may be of good service to you! He is the one to go to Boozan Island. He can steal the Princess to be your bride. Then, should her father declare war upon us, it will take him ten years of sailing to get here. But a lot can happen in ten years. I heard once that somewhere some wizard promised some king that within ten years he would teach a horse to sing like a nightingale."

"By my crown, you are right!" cried Douda. "Thanks to you, Fool! As reward I shall order another bell to be sewed on your cap and a cookie given to each of your children."

The Jester was pleased because he took great pride in the little bells and, to show his appreciation, he stood on his head.

Now, by the King's command, the heavy iron doors were opened, and the seventh Simeon was led out and brought before the King.

"Certainly I can steal the Princess," said Simeon. "It shouldn't be much trouble. She is not a precious pearl kept under seven locks. Order, Douda, the ship to be loaded with fine cloths and ivory, with Persian rugs and precious stones. Then I and my brothers will sail to Boozan Island and bring back the beautiful Princess to be your bride."

There was great hustle and bustle in the kingdom. By the King's order the ship was loaded and in less time than it takes to braid the hair on a bald man's head, the brothers said good-bye and were off.

Their ship sailed upon the waters of the Great Sea. Its carved prow cut the waves like a sharp plow. Then before they had time to say "What a jolly good ride," in the distant blue, Boozan Island appeared to the brothers' view.

They saw Boozan Island, all black with bristling guns. The great

armies were marching all over it to the beating of drums. The King's spare army was there too, being fed and groomed. From their high tower the King's sentries spied the ship and cried out with loud voice, "Hold, drop the anchor! Answer us! Who are you and why do you come here?"

The seventh Simeon replied, "We are peaceful merchants and bear no arms. We have fine cloths and ivory, Persian rugs and precious stones. And what we sell is not dear. For a mouse's tail you can buy a whale! Besides, we have nice presents for your King."

When the King heard of it, he ordered the Simeons brought to his royal palace. The brothers loaded up a little boat with what they had, and came ashore as they were told.

In the great hall of the royal palace the Boozan King was sitting on a throne with Princess Helena by his side. So lovely she was that her beauty could not be imagined or described or told about in a tale. She had golden hair, rosy cheeks, and eyes so sweet, so gentle, that if you saw her, all you could say would be, "Oh, how beautiful is the Princess!"

But the seventh Simeon said, "We are peaceful merchants from beyond the sea. We came here to sell, to buy, and to trade. And we brought a few little presents for Your Majesty, should you honor us by their acceptance."

Saying this he bowed low and his brothers unrolled their precious cloths of most luscious quality, and rare velvets, quite priceless. They spread out the marvels of carved ivory and round pearls. Rich cloaks, sewed with gold, all gold, solid gold. They sparkled like fire! Bracelets, earrings, necklaces, diamonds, rubies, and sapphires.

When she saw the treasures the Princess clapped her hands, exclaiming with delight, "Aren't they lovely! Many thanks to you, dear strangers, for your beautiful gifts."

"Oh, but no!" answered the seventh Simeon. "Those are just trifles for you to give to your servants. The cloths are for the chambermaids to use as rags and the round pearls for the kitchen boys to play marbles with. We do have real treasures too, but being afraid of not pleasing Your Majesty, we left them on our ship. If only, wise beautiful Princess, you would honor us by coming to our ship to see and to choose for yourself, you could have all and the ship itself as well. What good to us are all the jewels in the world after we've seen your lovely eyes?"

The Princess was pleased with his simple words and she asked her father, "Father dear, may I go? I shall see and choose for myself and bring back something for you, too."

The Boozan King thought awhile and then he said, "Well, dear

daughter, if you must, you must. But you shall go there on my royal ship which has a hundred guns on it, with one hundred of the Best Warriors and a thousand other soldiers, just in case something should happen."

The royal ship left the shore. Upon it were many of the Best Warriors and other soldiery and one hundred guns. When they reached the Simeons' ship, the Princess went aboard it, climbing up its crystal stairs. The seventh Simeon led her from cabin to cabin, from one hold to another, showing her everything and telling her stories. And the stories he told her were so good that beautiful Helena forgot the time.

But the fourth Simeon had not forgotten. He took the ship by its carved prow, he made it go down and he hid it deep down below in the watery depths. The Best Warriors, when they saw this, bellowed like bulls, and the thousand other soldiers hung their heads and only stood blinking and looking into the water. Then, because there was nothing they could do, they turned the royal ship back to shore and went to tell the King of this unexpected, unheard-of misfortune.

The Boozan King when he heard of it cried bitterly, saying, "Oh, my dear beautiful daughter! God has punished me for my stubborn pride. I thought there was no king or prince worthy of your hand, and I guarded you like a precious jewel. But now you lie dead in the watery depths among seaweed and coral." Then he turned to the Best Warriors. "And you, you blockheads, why didn't you look? Off to jail with you while I think of a punishment so severe that even your children and grandchildren will remember it!"

While the Boozan King raved and lamented, the brothers' ship was streaking under the water like a silver fish. Then, with the island left far behind them, the fourth Simeon brought it up again to sail upon the calm blue waters of the sea.

But the Princess began to think of the time. "I must go home. If I don't go very soon my father might become angry." As she said this she came up on deck and lo, there was no Boozan Island! Only the blue sea around and the blue sky above. Now it would seem the rest would be easy—the brothers had their prize and were sailing home. But no—there is more to this story!

The Princess knew some magic. She raised up her hands, looked to the sky, and turned into a beautiful bird of many colors. She spread her wings and flew away. Here the fifth Simeon lost no time. He loaded his gun with a silver bullet, aimed—bang! And the bird fell down, shot in the wing. But before it reached the water the sixth Simeon caught it in his hands. Then the bird turned into a little silver fish and slipped out into the deep water. Simeon caught the

fish too, but in his very hands it turned into a little gray mouse and went running around the deck. But Simeon pounced on it quicker than a cat, and in his hands the little mouse became the beautiful Princess once more, and this time for good. Because this was all the magic the beautiful Princess knew.

It was early, early in the morning when King Douda sat at the crystal window of his palace, thinking. "Could the brothers bring the Princess? Would the brothers come back at all?" And he gazed upon the blue waters of the sea lost in thought. He could not sleep, he could not eat, or go hunting, or join a feast. The beautiful Princess was on his mind.

King Douda looked upon the waters. "What is it there? Is it a white gull flying or a ship sailing?" Yes! It was the brothers' ship flying home. The flags waving, silken sails blown full by the wind, and good music played by the sailors upon its rigging.

The signal gun boomed from the shore. Now the ship drew nearer and dropped anchor. Its sails were furled, a plank was laid ashore and the Princess came off the ship. She was as beautiful as the bright sun in the morning, as lovely as the heavenly stars of the night!

King Douda rejoiced when he saw her. "Run," he said, "all my Sergeants, Lieutenants, Major-Generals and the Best People, fire the cannons, blow the trumpets, and sound the bells! Run, greet the Princess, your future queen."

They all ran to do as they were told and spread the precious carpets and opened wide the gates. Even the King himself ran out to welcome Helena to his kingdom. He took her by the hands and led her to his palace, saying, "Please, my beautiful Helena, make yourself at home. We have heard about your beauty but truly it is greater than we had hoped. But, if you say the word, I shall send you back to your dear father. I cannot be so cruel as to keep you here by force!"

Here the Princess looked upon King Douda and, as she looked at him, it seemed to her as if the sun itself danced in the sky, as if the sea played music and the mountains broke out in a song!

What more can one say? The Princess saw how good-looking Douda was and she fell in love with him.

It was not long thereafter that the seven Simeons were sent back to the Boozan King bearing a letter from his daughter, Helena. She

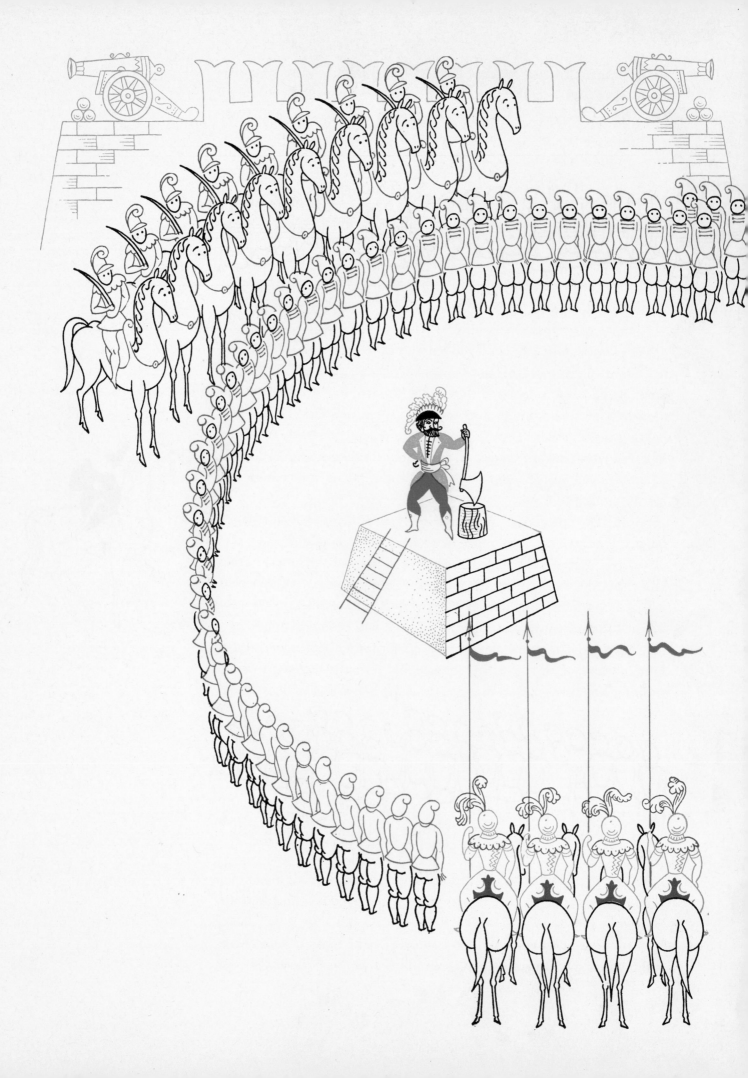

wrote, "Our King and my dear Father: I have found the man worthy of my hand and I shall marry him so soon as we have your blessing. The High and Mighty King Douda, my future husband and your son-in-law, sends to you his envoys with greetings and best wishes. And we both hope that you will come to our wedding."

They sailed swiftly beyond the sea and in less time than it takes to tell about it the seven brothers reached Boozan Island. The King's great armies were assembled upon a big square. In the middle of the square rose a scaffold and on the scaffold stood the King's headsman holding a shiny axe. The King had ordered put to death all of the Best Warriors and the thousand other soldiers who had guarded his daughter. "Chop off their heads!" he said. "All of them, from the first to the last!"

"Stop! Do not chop!" cried the seventh Simeon from the ship's poop. "We have brought you a letter from your daughter."

So delighted was the Boozan King when he read the letter that he said, "Let the fools go. I forgive them. It must have been God's own will that my dear daughter should marry King Douda."

The brothers were given a great feast and sent back with the King's blessing for the wedding. He himself could not go because of important matters of state which required his direct attention, such as training his army and seeing that his spare army was well groomed.

Faster than before, the brothers sailed back towards their own home. In no time, in the distant blue, King Douda's kingdom appeared in their view.

"Our thanks to you, my good fellows," said King Douda cheerfully, when the Simeons stood before him and the Princess. "It was

well done and we are both very happy. Now you can ask for anything you desire. Should you like to be my generals, I shall make you my Field Marshals. But should you rather be my Senators, I shall make you my Prime Ministers. Then you can have all the gold and silver you need."

The first brother bowed low before the King and replied, "We seven brothers are only simple folk and your peasants, Douda. It is not for us to strut at the Royal Court. We shouldn't know when to stand up or when to sit down, or what to wear and when! But give us leave to go back to our field. By us it was plowed and by us seeded and now its golden wheat shines in the sun. One thing we beg of you. Let our seventh brother go with us. Forgive him his talent. He is not the first to have it nor will he be the last!"

"Be it so," said the King. "But we are very sorry you cannot stay for our wedding. It's going to be such a fine party!"

The wedding day soon arrived and there was great merriment and joy in the land. Good King Douda married the Princess Helena and they both were so good-looking that all the people cheered and cried, "Hurrah!"

The church bells pealed, the flags waved and the cannons fired the salutes until they burst.

It was a fine party! I should know because I was there myself and danced to the gay music till I couldn't dance any more!

And now, my gentle friends, we are at the tale's end. For what was good in it, praise it; but for the rest forgive the poor story-teller. A wrong word is not like the bird in a cage. If ever a word flies out, no man can jump and catch it. In this I have no doubt!

# DATE DUE

| OCT 2 4 1990 | | |
|---|---|---|
| OCT 2 8 1991 | | |
| OCT 1 2 1992 | | |
| | | |
| | | |
| | | |
| | | |
| | | |
| | | |
| | | |
| | | |
| | | |
| | | |
| | | |
| | | |
| GAYLORD | | PRINTED IN U.S.A. |